STANLEY'S PLAN

Ruth Green

Tate Publishing

Stanley the dog is
ALWAYS hungry.

'That smells so delicious,'
Stan says to himself,
'But I'll never reach it
up there on the shelf.'

So Stanley starts
to make a plan.
He asks Brian the cat
to help if he can.

'I could climb
on a chair,
right on my tip toes,
I'll stretch very tall
with a mouse
on my nose.'

'It just won't work, Stan,'
said Sid the snail.
'The chair is too wobbly,
you're going to fail.'

'The birds have flown off
to a cherry tree,'
said Herbert the hedgehog.
'They'll be home for tea.'

Now Stanley is more
hungry than ever.
He asks Owl for some help,
because owls are clever.

But Owl just hoots and says,
'Wait and see,'
And Stanley goes to sleep,
he's as tired as can be.

All of the animals each
have a slice.
'What a treat,' says Stanley,
'Aren't birthdays nice?'

First published 2015 by order of the Tate Trustees
by Tate Publishing, a division of Tate Enterprises Ltd,
Millbank, London SW1P 4RG
www.tate.org.uk/publishing

A catalogue record for this book is available
from the British Library
ISBN 978-1-84976-305-9

Distributed in the United States and Canada
by ABRAMS, New York
Library of Congress Control Number applied for

Typeset by Jason Godfrey
Colour reproduction by Evergreen Colour
Management Ltd, Hong Kong
Printed in China by Toppan Leefung Printing Ltd

MIX
Paper from
responsible sources
FSC® C104723
FSC
www.fsc.org